Three Billy Goats Gruff

illustrated by Alison Edgson

Child's Play (International) Ltd

Ashworth Rd, Bridgemead, Swindon, SN5 7YD UK

Swindon   Auburn ME   Sydney

© 2005 Child's Play (International) Ltd   Printed in Guangzhou, China

ISBN 978-1-904550-72-3   Z111213FUFT0314723

13 15 17 19 20 18 16 14

www.childs-play.com

Once upon a time,
there were three Billy Goats,
each called 'Gruff'.

They lived in a valley in the winter to keep warm.
When spring came, they climbed
up to the meadow on the hillside,
to eat the lush green grass that was there.

The path to the meadow
went across an old stone bridge
above a cool mountain stream.

Under this bridge lived
a mean and ugly troll,
with eyes as big as saucers,
ears as sharp as knives,
and a nose as long as a poker.

This troll was always hungry,
and slept most of the time.

When he was awake,
he bullied the other creatures
who lived under the bridge.

One Spring day, the youngest
of the Billy Goats Gruff decided
that it was time to go to the hillside meadow.
Off she trotted, up the path and onto the bridge.
'Trip-trap-trip-trap' went her hooves on the bridge,
waking the troll from his sleep.

"Who's that trip-trapping on my bridge?!" roared the troll. "Just me!" called out the youngest Billy Goat Gruff. "I'm going up to the meadow on the hill to eat and eat! I'm really hungry!"

"I'm really hungry, too," snarled the troll.
"And I'm bigger than you.

I'm going to have to gobble you up
for my breakfast."

"Don't be silly, you big, ugly troll,"
replied the youngest Billy Goat Gruff.
"I'm much too small, not even a proper mouthful.
Why don't you wait for the second Billy Goat Gruff?
He's big enough for lunch as well as breakfast!"

"Well," said the troll, scratching his head.
"That's an idea. Be off with you!"
And the youngest Billy Goat Gruff
went skipping up the hillside.

By this time, the second Billy Goat Gruff had also decided to climb up the hillside to the lush meadow. 'Trip-trap-trip-trap -trip-trap-trip-trap' went his hooves on the bridge.

"Who's that trip-trip-trip-trap-trap-trapping on my bridge?!" roared the troll.
"It's just me, you big, ugly troll!" called out the second Billy Goat Gruff.
"I'm going up to the meadow on the hill to eat and eat and eat! I'm really, really, really hungry!"

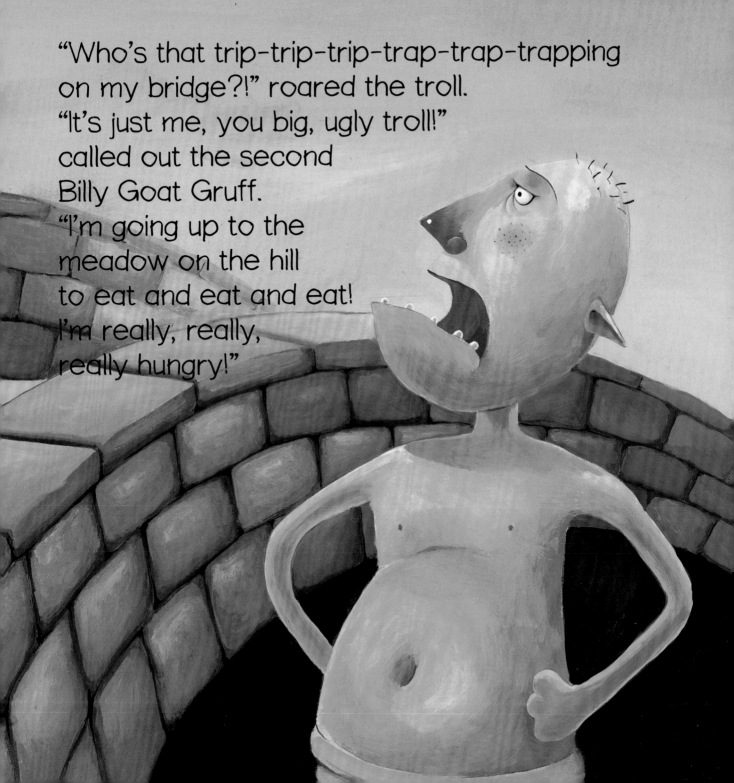

"I'm really, really, really hungry, too,"
snarled the troll.
"And I'm bigger than you – well, just about.
So I'm going to have to gobble you up instead."

"Don't waste your time,"
said the second Billy Goat Gruff.

"You should eat the third Billy Goat Gruff.
He is big enough for breakfast,
lunch and dinner rolled into one!"

The troll scratched his head again.
All this thinking instead of just growling
was difficult. "Well," he said, "Maybe I will.
Be off with you before I change my mind!"

And the second Billy Goat Gruff
went running off up the hillside.

All of a sudden the earth began to shake.

The troll thought it might be an earthquake,
but it was the biggest Billy Goat Gruff
walking up to the bridge. He was ENORMOUS!

'TRIP-TRAP-TRIP-TRAP-TRIP-TRAP-TRIP-TRAP'
went his huge hooves on the bridge,
'TRIP-TRAP-TRIP-TRAP-TRIP-TRAP-TRIP-TRAP.'
The bridge creaked and groaned under the weight.

"What a noise!" said the troll,
in his meanest voice.
"You must be the big Billy Goat Gruff.
I've never seen so much food in one goat!"

The big Billy Goat Gruff looked down at the troll.
"And you must be the little troll
that's been such a nuisance," he thundered.

"Yes," replied the troll,
"And I'm going to gobble you up!"

"I don't think so,"
laughed the big Billy Goat Gruff.
"But I'm too busy to fight now.
If I don't get up onto the hillside,
there'll be no grass left.
I'll deal with you when I get back in the winter."

And he went lumbering off up the hillside.

The three Billy Goats Gruff spent all Summer
on the hillside, eating enough grass
to last them through the winter...

...and, to be truthful,
some of next Spring as well.

The troll was secretly very glad that
the big Billy Goat Gruff had not stayed to fight.
He quietly packed his bags and left for good,
well before the winter came.